They found their seats. They clicked their safety belts into place.

"Don't worry," said Tom. "I know what happens on aeroplanes. I'll help you."

"Thank you, Tom. After we've taken off, I'll tell you about my first flying adventure," said Grandma, winking again. "And it won't be a fib!"

Chapter 2

Grandma's First Flight

The flight attendants walked up and down, checking everybody's safety belts. Then they showed everyone how to use the safety equipment and where the exits were, in case there was an emergency.

With a bump, the plane started to move. It taxied out to the runway, and the jet engines roared.

The aeroplane sped down the runway. A few minutes later, Tom and his grandmother were high above the clouds. Tom turned to Grandma.

"What happened on your first aeroplane flight, Grandma?" he asked. "Was it before I was born?"

"Oh, it was a long time before you were born," replied Grandma. She started counting on her fingers and then laughed.

"Over sixty years before you were born, in fact."

Tom looked amazed. "I didn't know they *had* aeroplanes that long ago," he said.

"Oh, yes," replied his grandmother. She looked around the aeroplane. "But they looked very different to this big jet," she said, smiling.

The flight attendant brought Grandma a cup of tea, and an orange juice for Tom.

Grandma sipped her tea, and began her story.

"Over sixty years ago, flying was still an adventure," she started. "Brave men and women would try to fly long distances in their small aeroplanes. There were no radar stations, satellites or control towers to help them find their way. They used compasses and maps, and flew low so they could see where they were."

"The jet engine hadn't been invented, so they flew slower than aeroplanes today. Because they were slow and flew low, they couldn't fly above the storm clouds. The pilots sat in noisy cockpits, where it was freezing cold. They flew the plane, checked all the engine gauges, and found their way, all at the same time. Flying was a dangerous and difficult thing to do in those days. But at least there were no *queues*," she said, winking.

"One day, when I was about your age, there was a story in the newspaper about a famous pilot. His name was Wilbur Addison and he was going to fly across the sea between Australia and New Zealand. The same trip we're flying now," she explained. "But in those days, the journey was long and dangerous. No-one flew between the two countries. Most people thought it couldn't be done."

"My brothers and I thought this was a very exciting adventure. We read all the newspaper stories about Wilbur. We imagined what it must feel like to fly across the sea. We wished we could have our own flying adventure."

Chapter 3

The Brave Pilot

"Before dawn, on the morning of Wilbur's flight to New Zealand, we sat around our radio for any news. We heard the crowd in Melbourne cheering as this brave pilot climbed in his aeroplane. Then his aeroplane, the *Tasman Flyer*, headed down the runway. The crowds cheered and waved."

"Then, everyone had to wait to see if this brave pilot would make it across the sea to New Zealand. That day, at school, we kept thinking about Wilbur Addison, wondering where he was."

"After school, we raced home and turned on the radio again. There had been no news about Wilbur."

"We listened to the radio, every half hour, until five o'clock. Everyone started to get worried. Surely, there should have been some news by now? What had happened to Wilbur and his aeroplane? No-one wanted to think that he might have crashed into the sea."

"At five-thirty, we sat around the radio, hoping for some good news. Then, we heard the most incredible news. The radio announcer was very excited. Soon, we were even more excited. Instead of landing in Auckland, as he was supposed to, someone had seen Wilbur flying towards *our* home town!"

"The radio announcer said he was expected to land at our airfield in the next half hour."

"You should have seen how fast we left the house! My brothers and I raced towards our bicycles, and we pedalled as fast as we could to the airfield. A crowd of people had already gathered there. They were all looking up at the sky, hoping to see Wilbur's aeroplane first. A few minutes later, someone shouted."

"'Look, over there!'"

"It was Wilbur's aeroplane! And it was flying right towards our airfield."

"As the aeroplane flew closer and lower, the crowd became silent. Everyone held their breath as the plane bumped and wobbled its way lower and lower. At last, its wheels touched down on the grassy airfield. The crowd let out a huge cheer! Wilbur Addison had arrived safely."

"The aeroplane taxied towards the crowd, and its engines slowed, then stopped. Wilbur pushed back his goggles and waved at us all. The crowd cheered again."

"Well, Tom, there was a lot of celebrating that night. Wilbur explained how he had been blown off course by the strong winds. And although he hadn't landed in Auckland, he had still landed— on the other side of the sea, in New Plymouth."

"That should have been enough excitement," laughed Grandma. "But there was more!"

She sipped her tea and, with a cheeky look on her face, pretended to look out the window. Tom couldn't wait to hear what else she had to say.

"Come on, Grandma!" he said excitedly. "What happened next?"

Chapter 4

Grandma's Lucky Ticket

Grandma laughed, and carried on with her story.

"The very next day, Wilbur was interviewed on the radio. He said that, as a thank-you to our town, he would take someone up in his aeroplane for a quick flight! There would be a raffle, and the tickets cost a penny each. My brothers and I took all the money we had, and rushed to the airfield to buy as many tickets as we could afford."

"I suppose you can guess who had the lucky ticket?" asked Grandma. Tom looked even more amazed.

"Yes, I was almost as amazed as you are now, Tom. And very scared, too! I had never been in a car, never mind an aeroplane. But I was not going to miss this adventure!" she said.

"That afternoon, I met Wilbur Addison. He smiled at me and shook my hand."

"Pleased to meet you, Miss," he said. "Are you ready for an adventure?"

By that time, I was too scared to speak, so I just nodded.

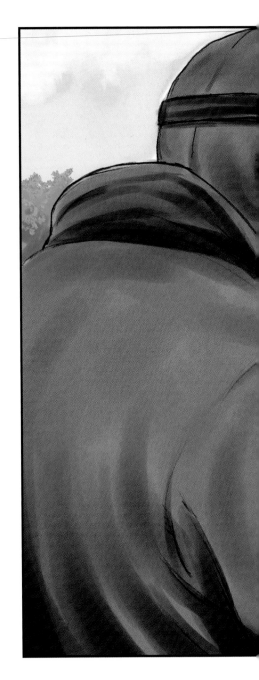

"We walked toward the aeroplane, and Wilbur helped me climb up into the cockpit. I had a bit of trouble getting up over the edge," laughed Grandma, remembering what had happened.

"Inside the cockpit, there were two tiny seats, one behind the other. It was tiny and very cramped. All around us were wires and dials and tools. Everything smelt of oil and fuel. I sat in the seat behind Wilbur's seat. He gave me a flying cap and goggles to put on. My first flight was about to begin!"

"Well, Tom, I am still amazed that I made it through the next ten minutes. Can you imagine your grandmother, sitting in a noisy, cold, cramped cockpit, smelling of oil and fuel, and racing down a bumpy airfield at a hundred kilometres an hour? And then, when we left the ground ..."

"That was the scariest moment of my life."

"The earth seemed to drop away below us. It felt like my tummy did, too! Within seconds, we were flying like a bird, high above the town."

"It was so exciting, I forgot to be scared. I couldn't believe how tiny the houses and roads looked from the aeroplane. I didn't even notice how cold and noisy it was up there. And then, all too soon, we glided towards the ground again. With a thud, we hit the grass, and rolled to a stop."

Chapter 5

A Fabulous Adventure

"Waiting for us was a crowd even bigger than yesterday. Everybody in town wanted to see the famous pilot and his aeroplane. And when we stood up, we heard another cheer. I felt very proud of myself!"

"Afterwards, Wilbur flew to Auckland, and then around the country to celebrate his famous flight. As for me ... well, you know what happened to me," said Grandma, chuckling. "I've had my feet firmly on the ground ever since," she laughed. "Until now, that is."

Tom stared at his grandmother and tried hard
to imagine her having such a fabulous adventure.
Could it really be true? Tom had hundreds of
questions he wanted to ask her, all at once.

Just as he had started to talk excitedly, the pilot's voice came over the aeroplane's radio.

"Ladies and gentlemen, this is your captain. Just to let you know that we're expecting a smooth flight across the Tasman Sea today. No turbulence, no strong winds, and a flying time of four hours. So please, relax and enjoy the food and the movie. Our flight attendants will be sure to make your journey an enjoyable one."

"That's more like it," said Grandma, taking off her shoes and closing her eyes. "This flight is going to be *much* more comfortable than the last one!"